Write-a-Story

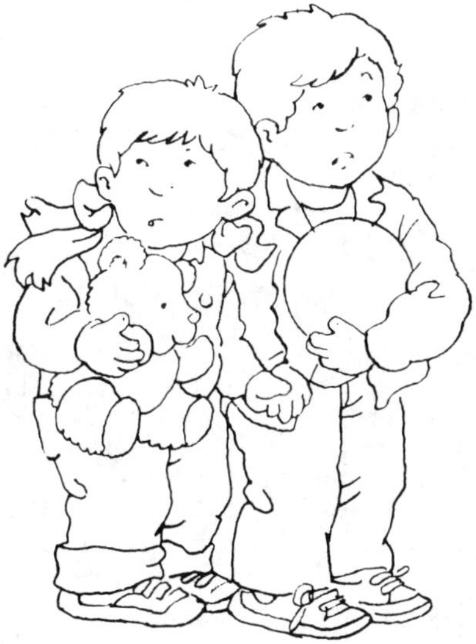

MOVING DAY

by ____________________

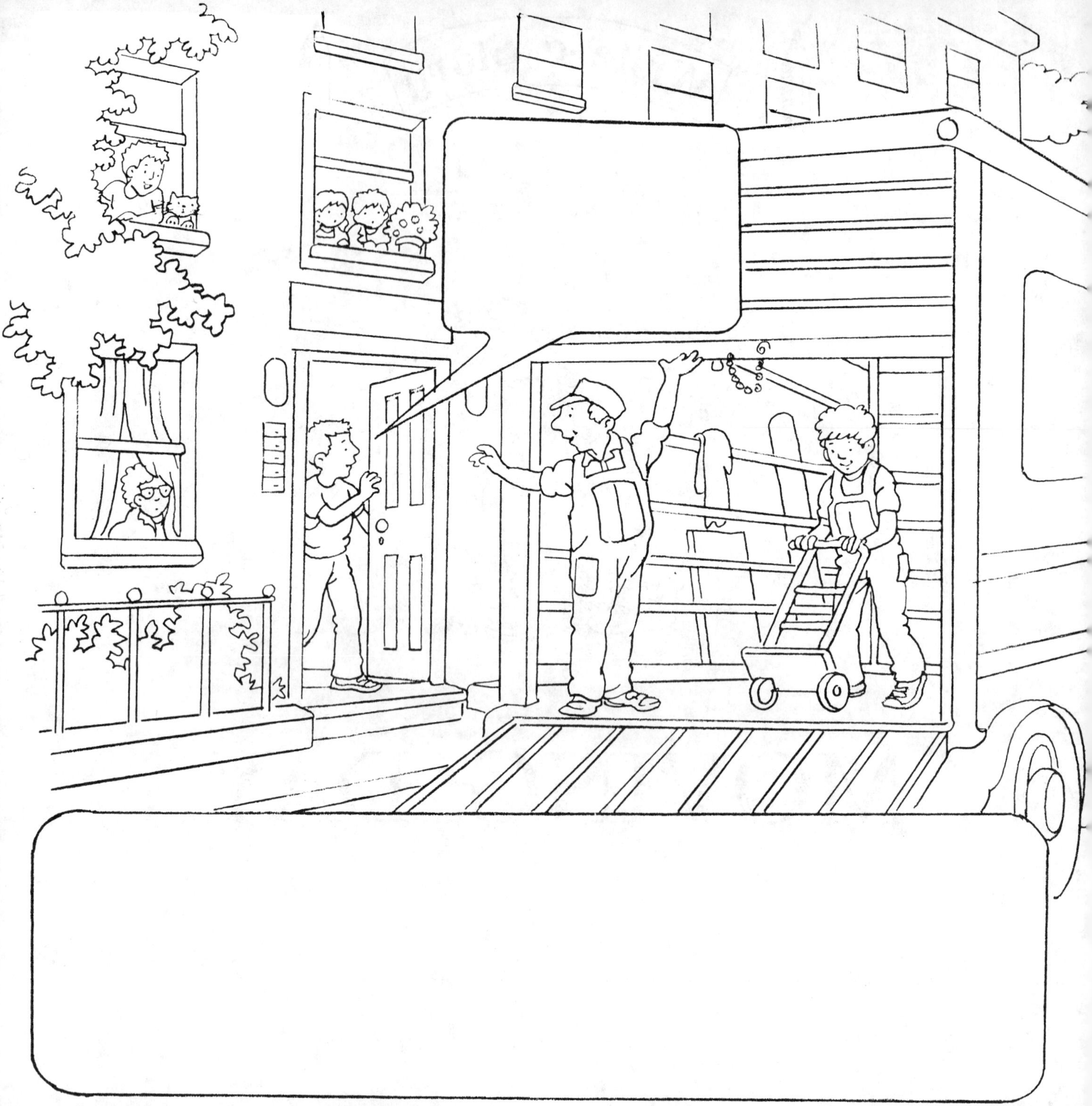

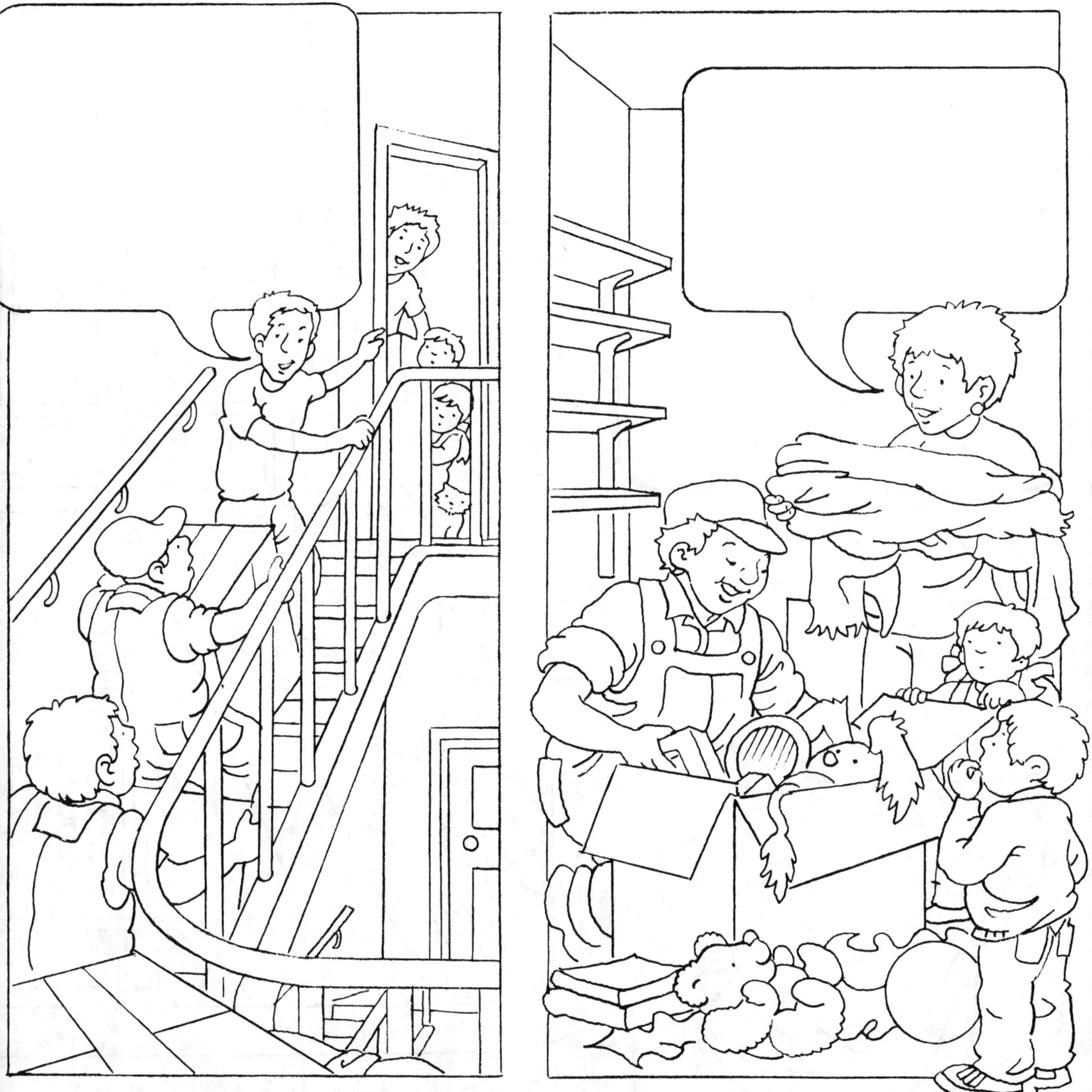

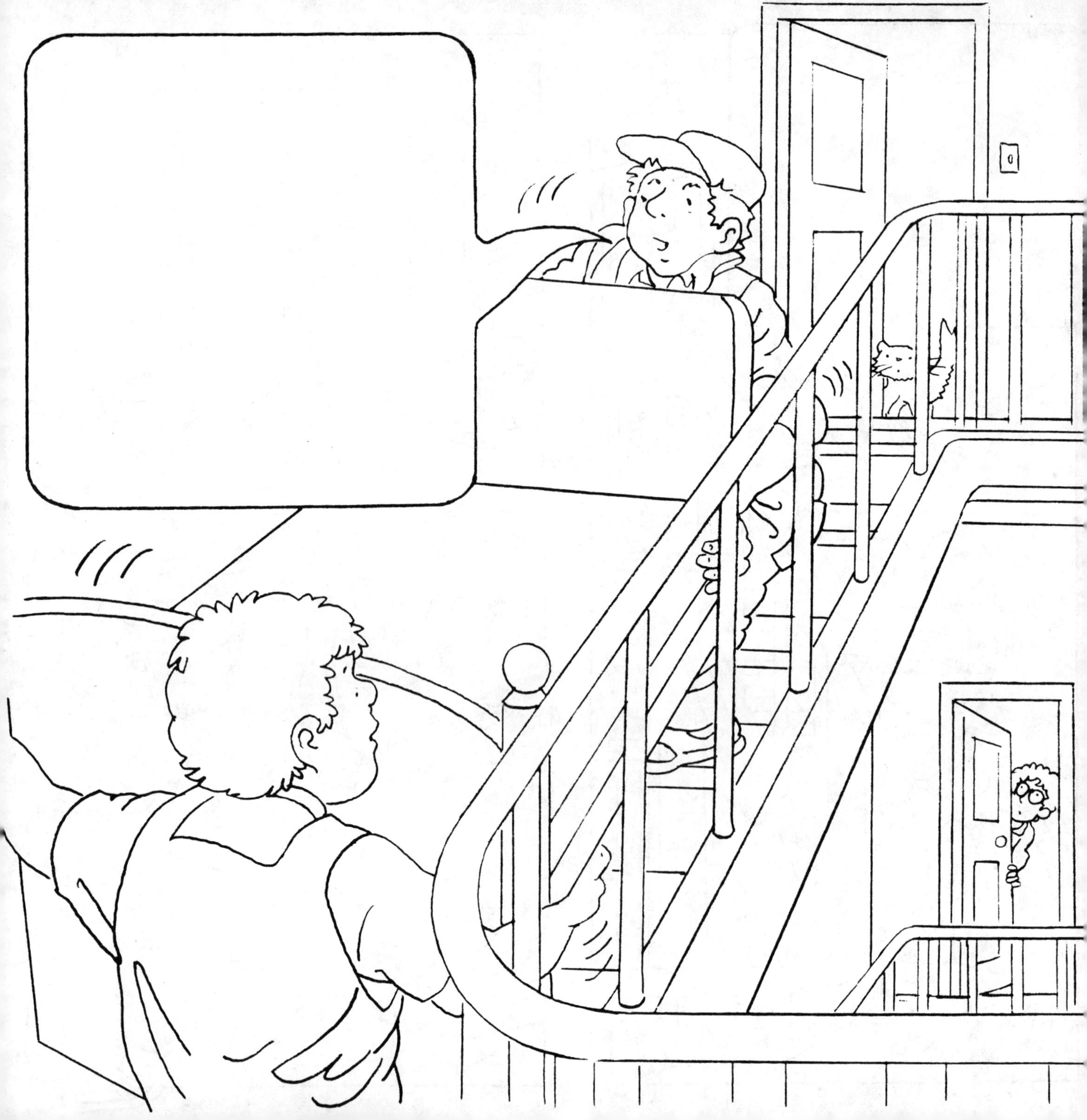

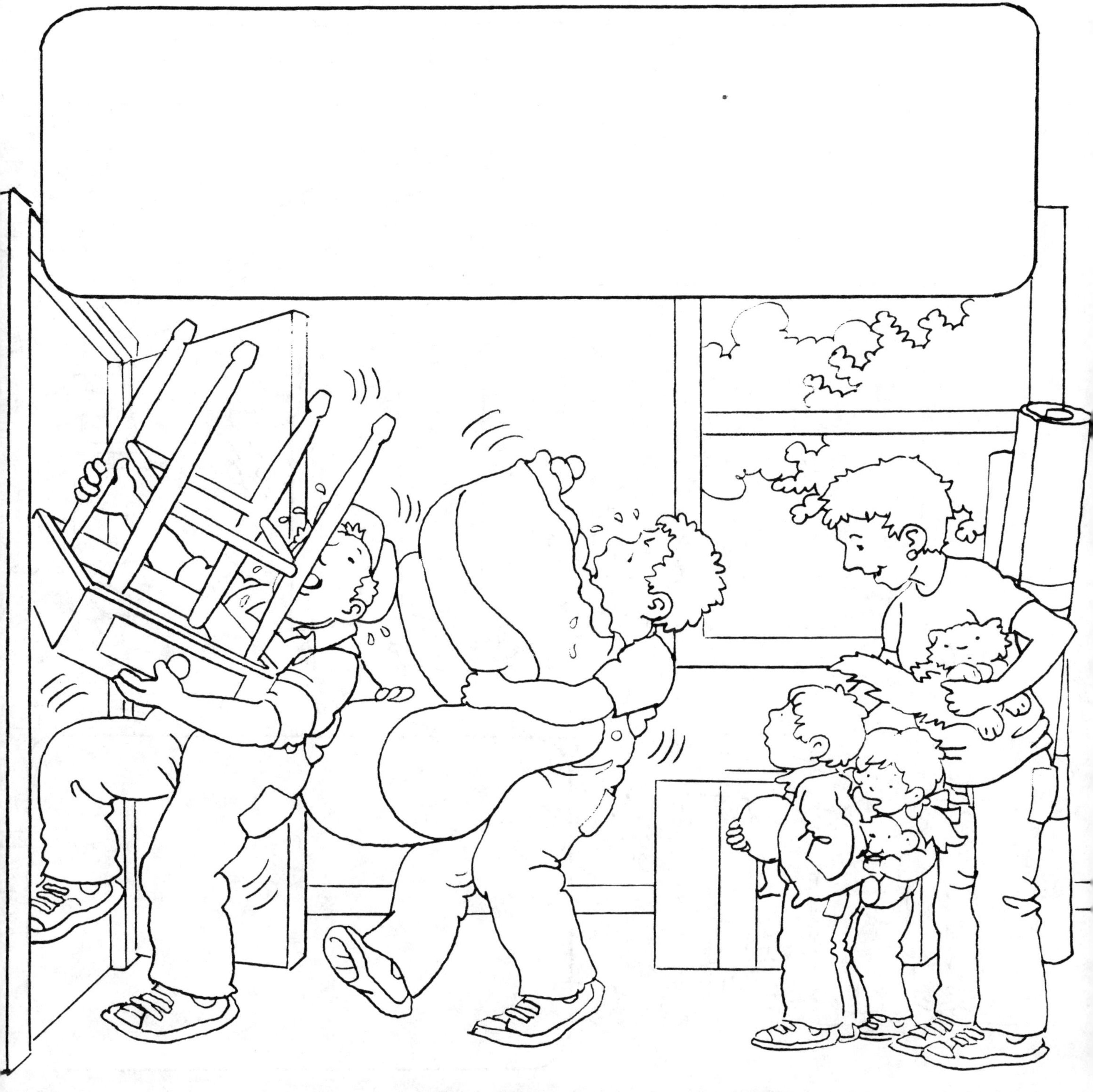

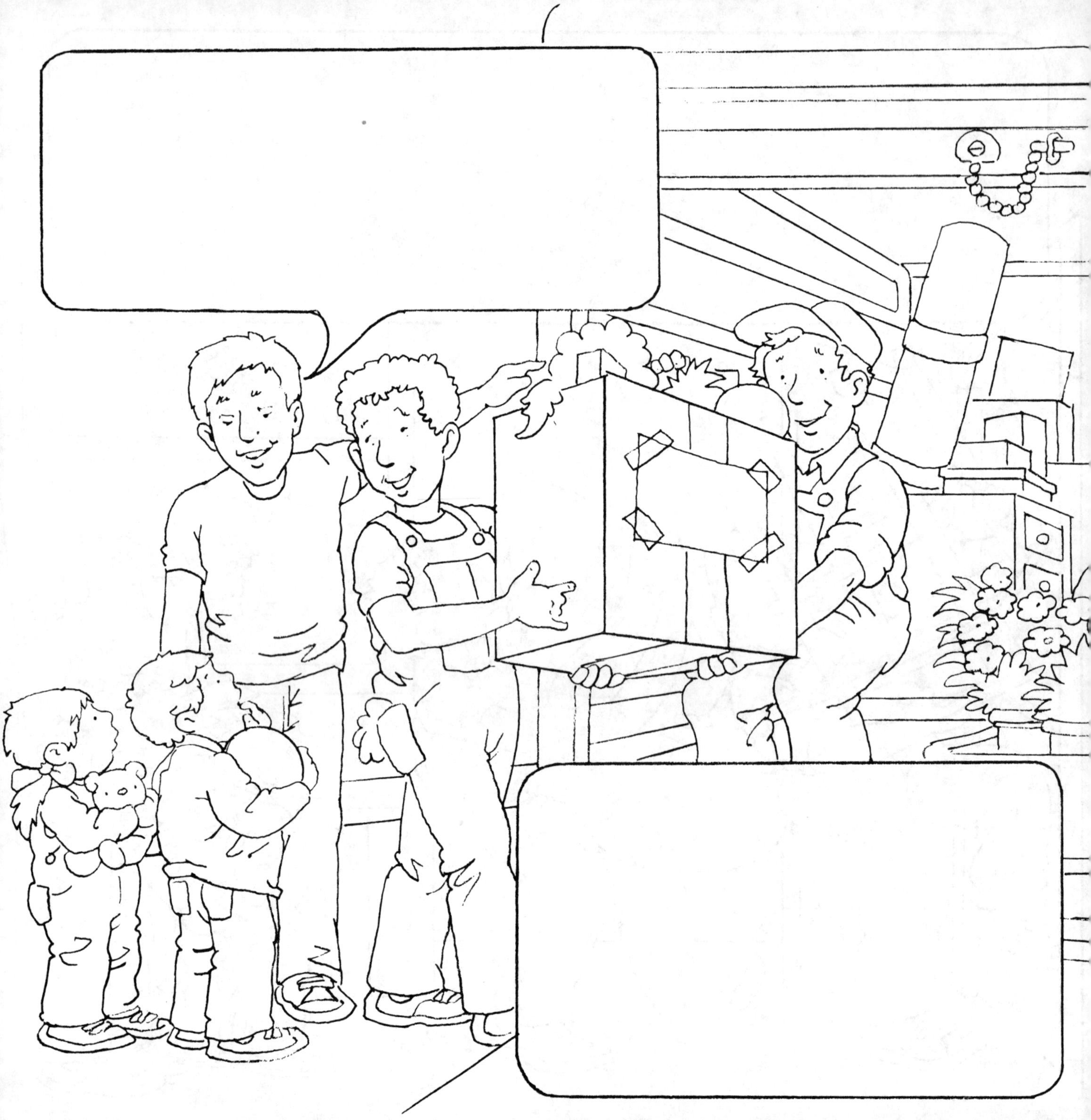

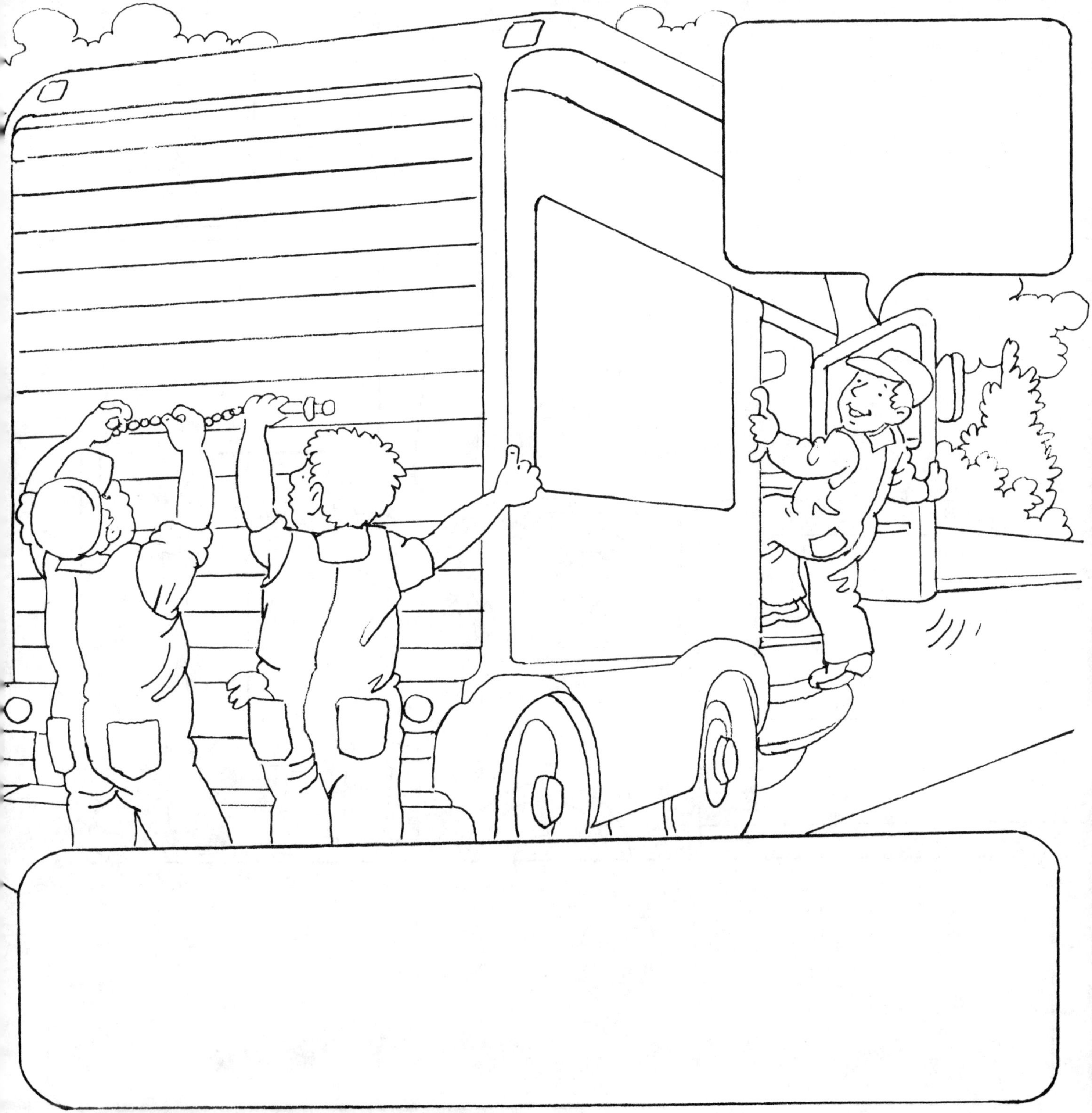

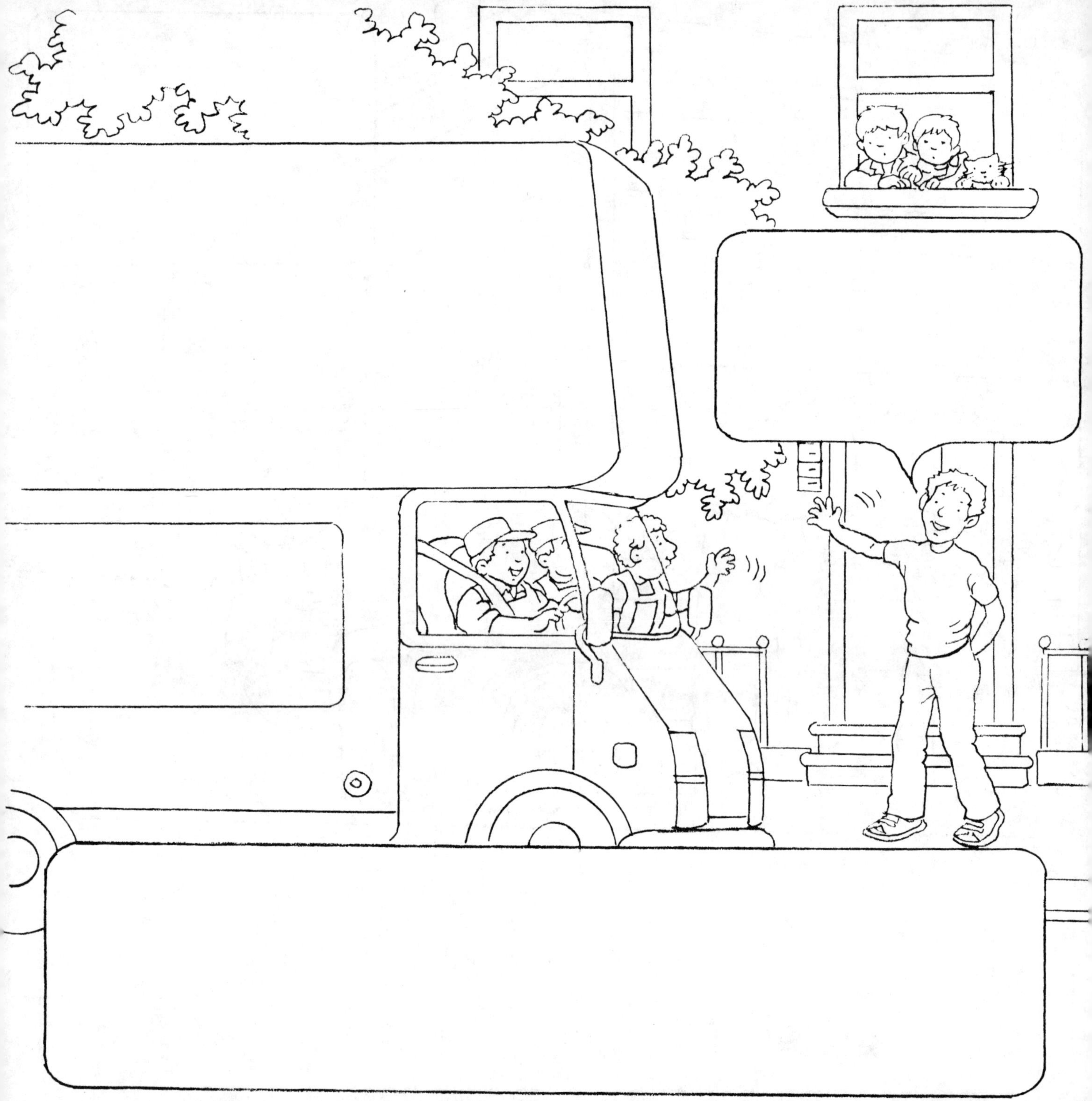

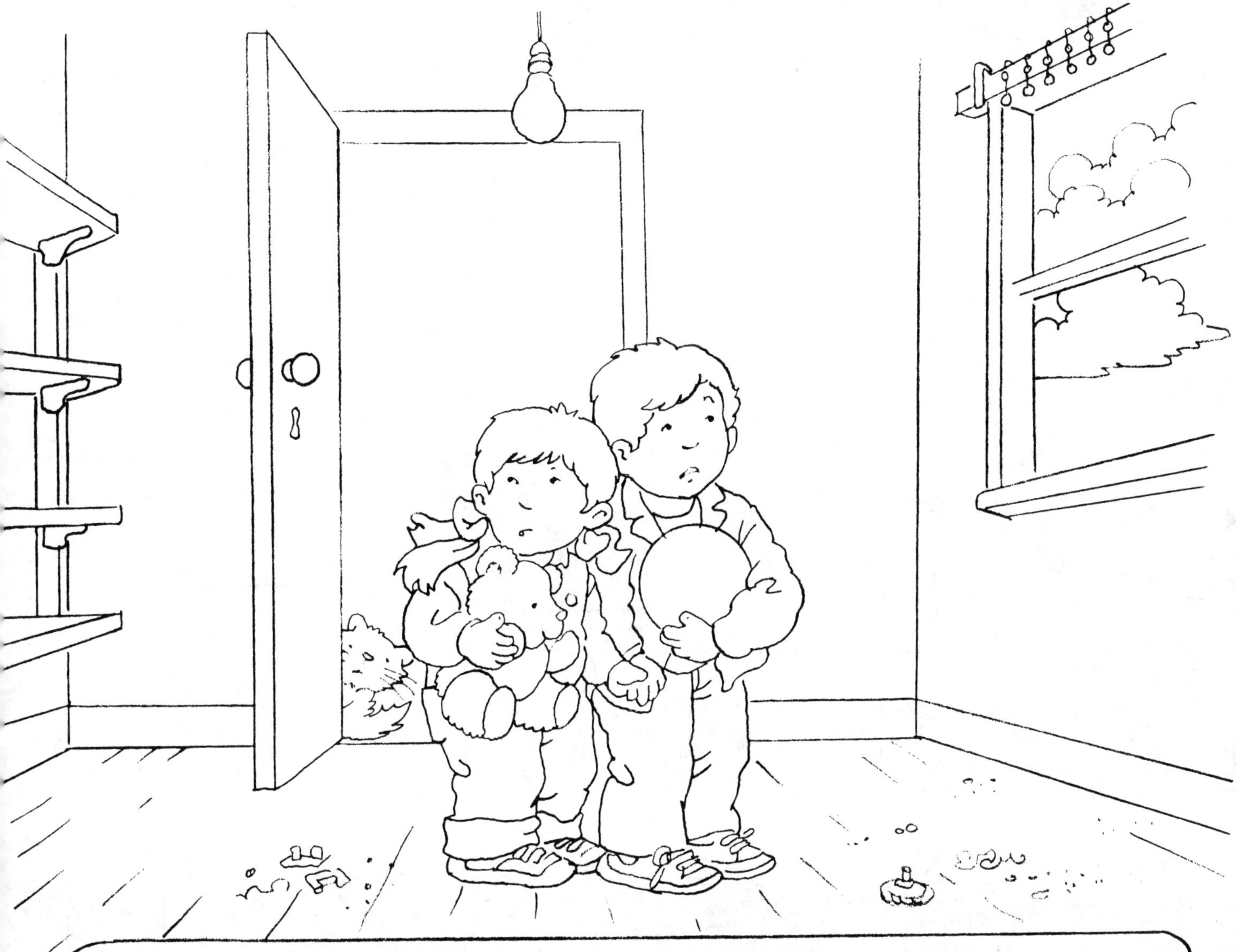

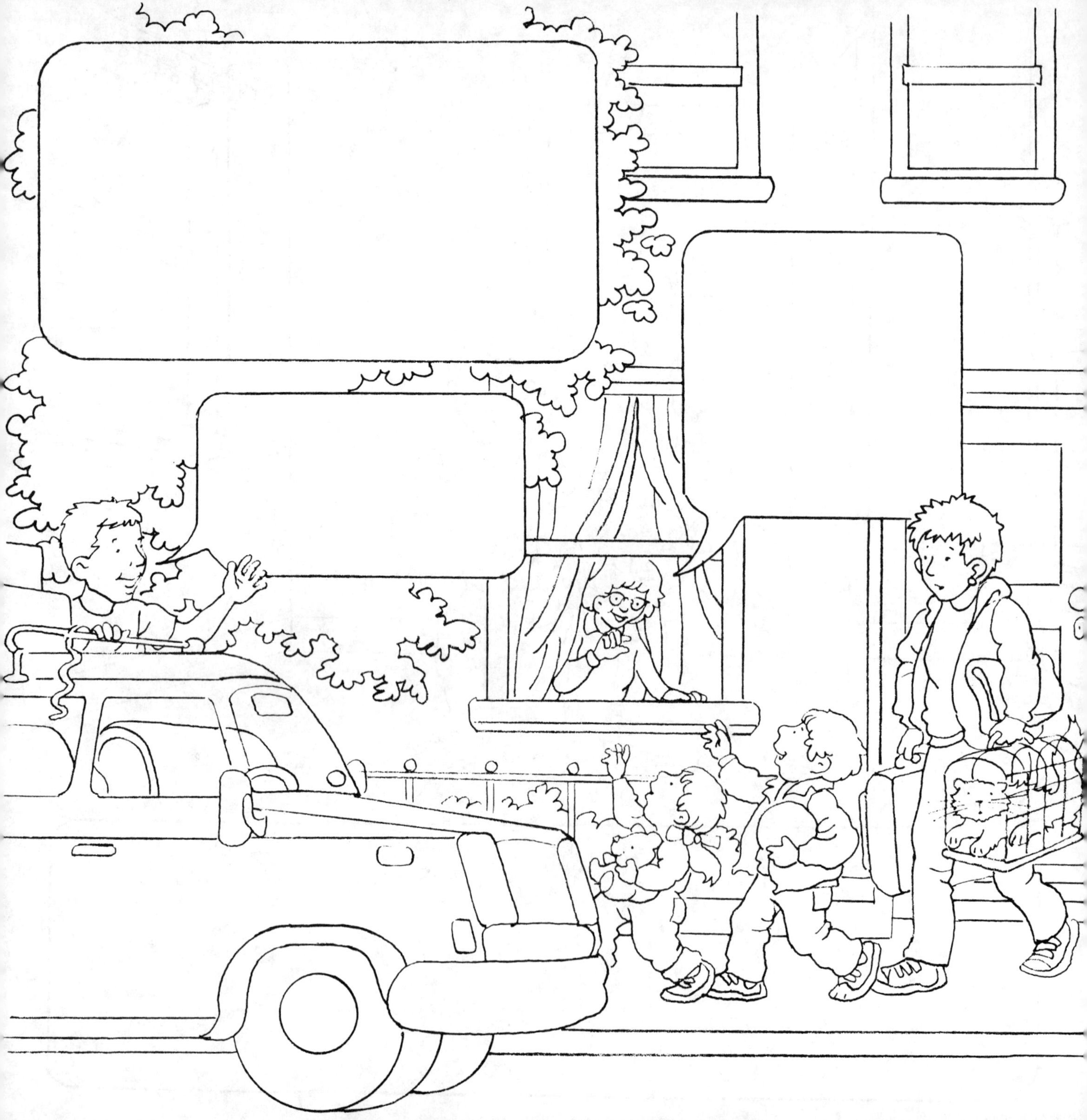

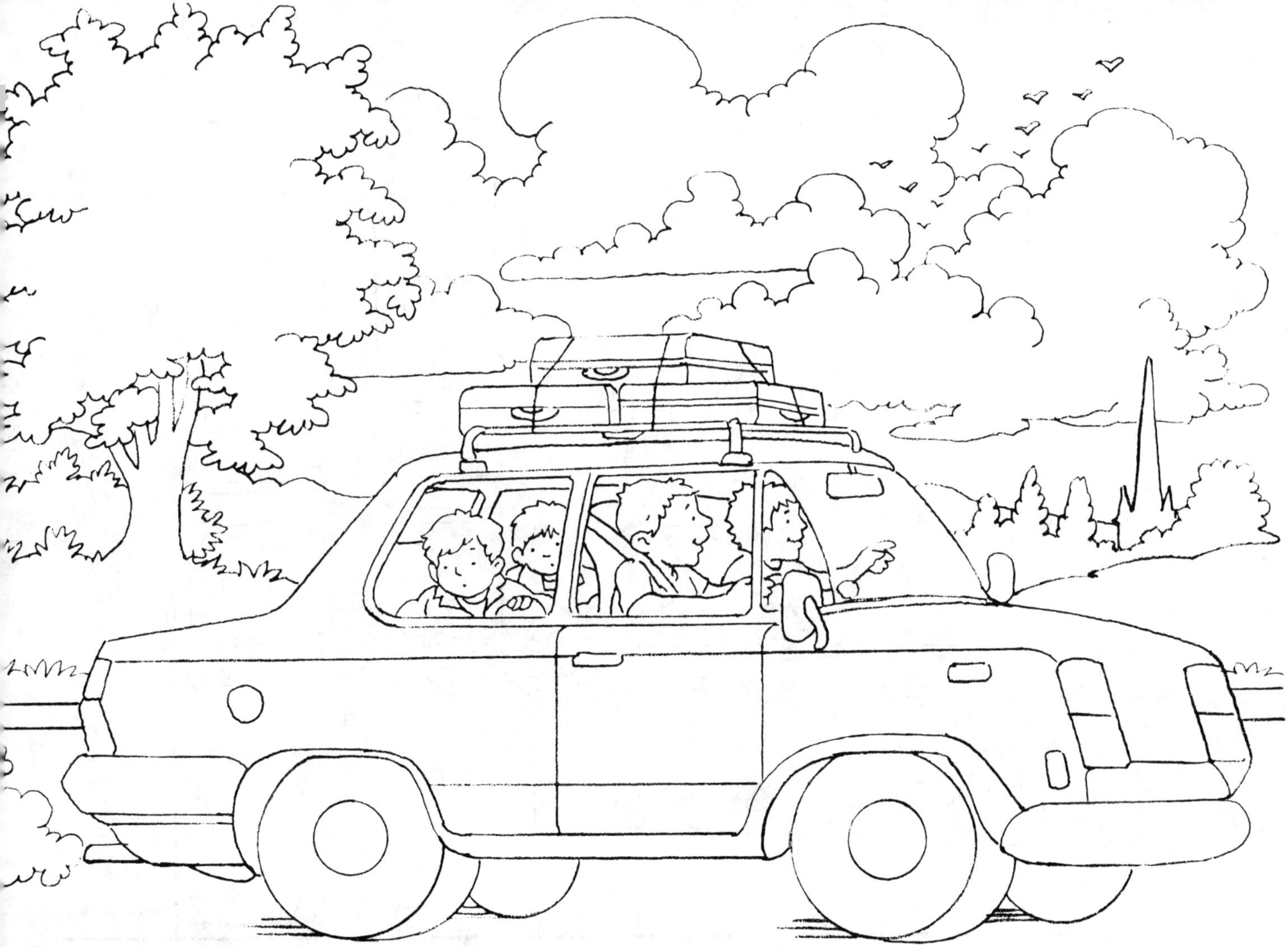

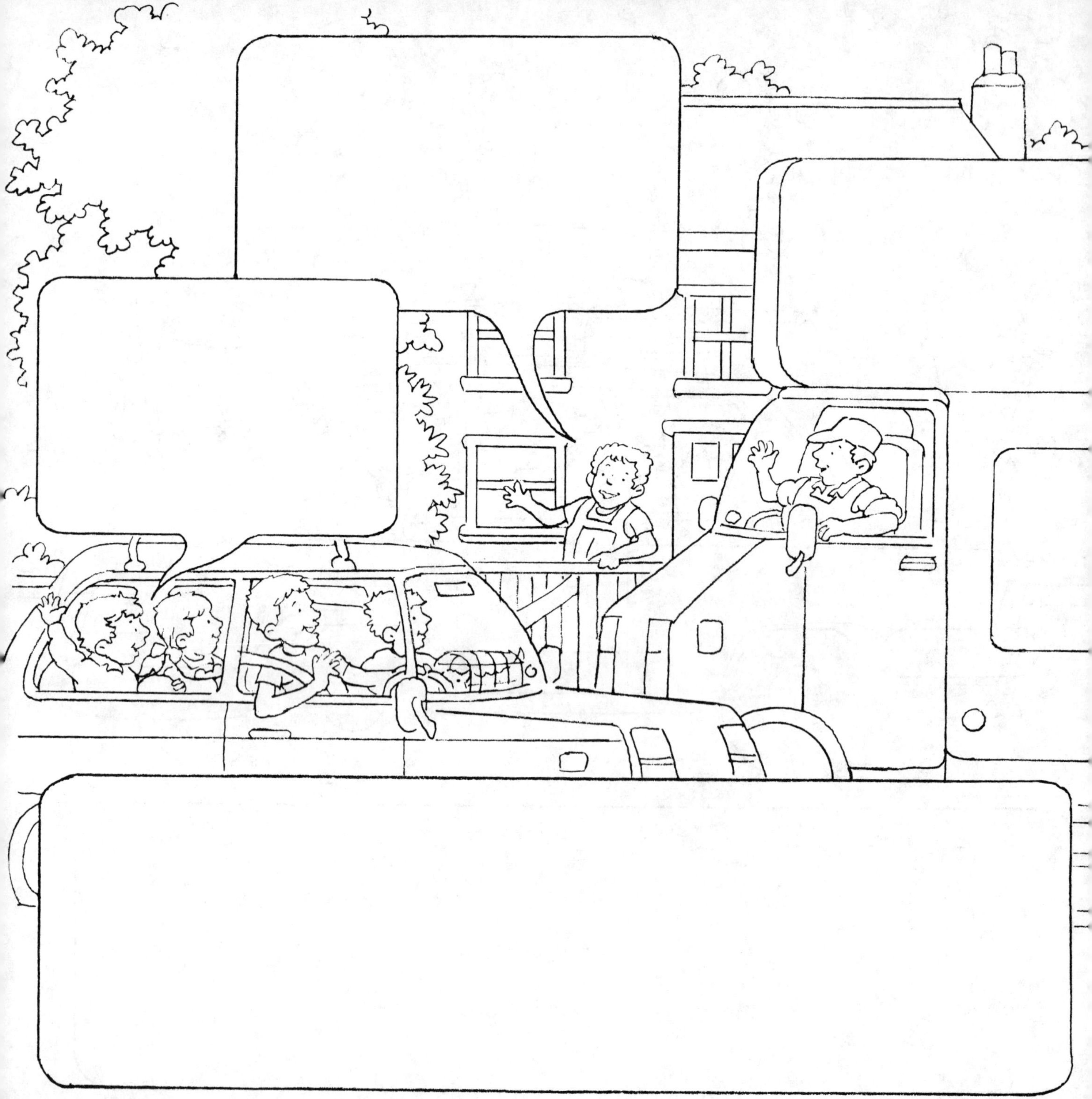

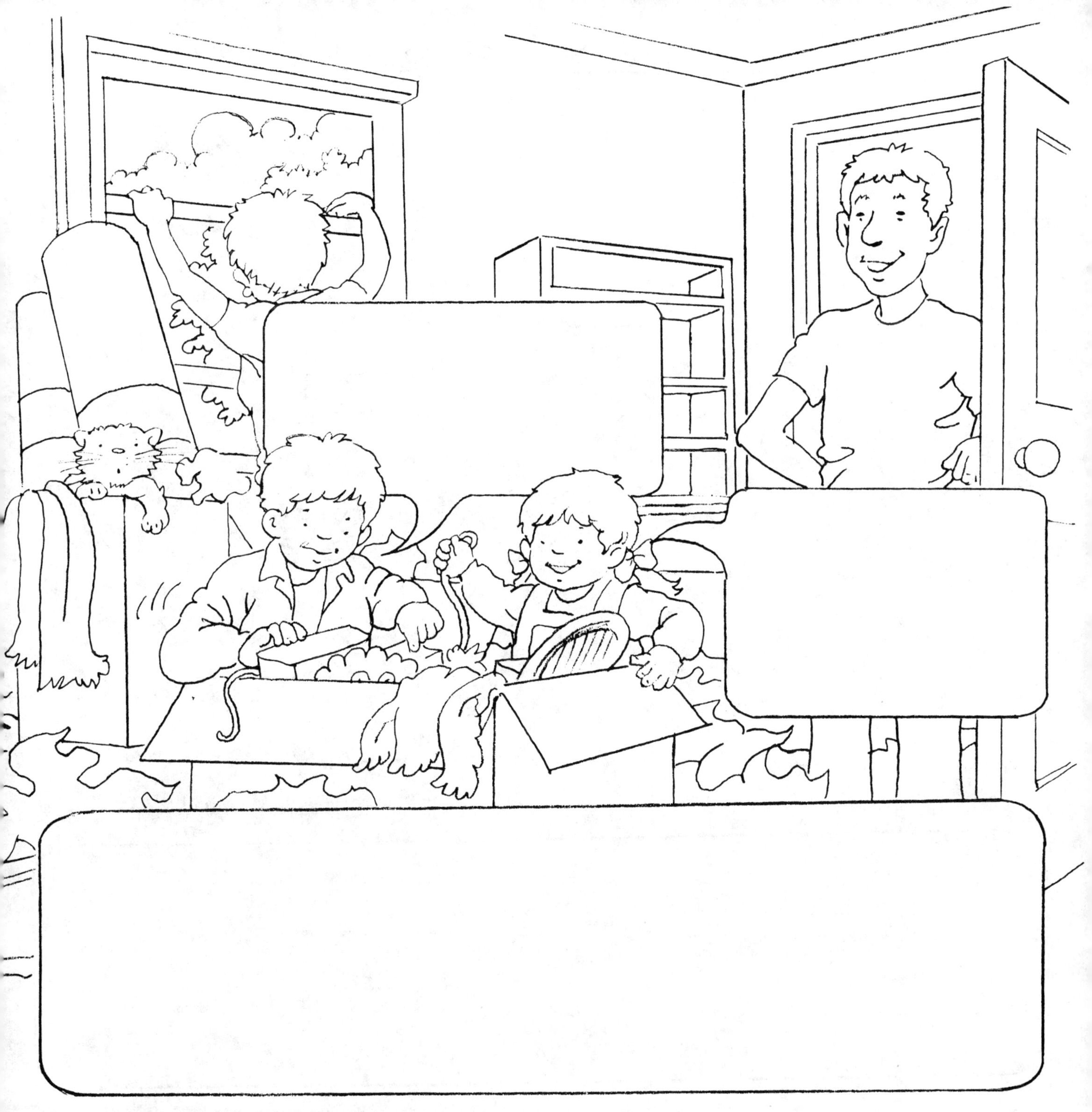

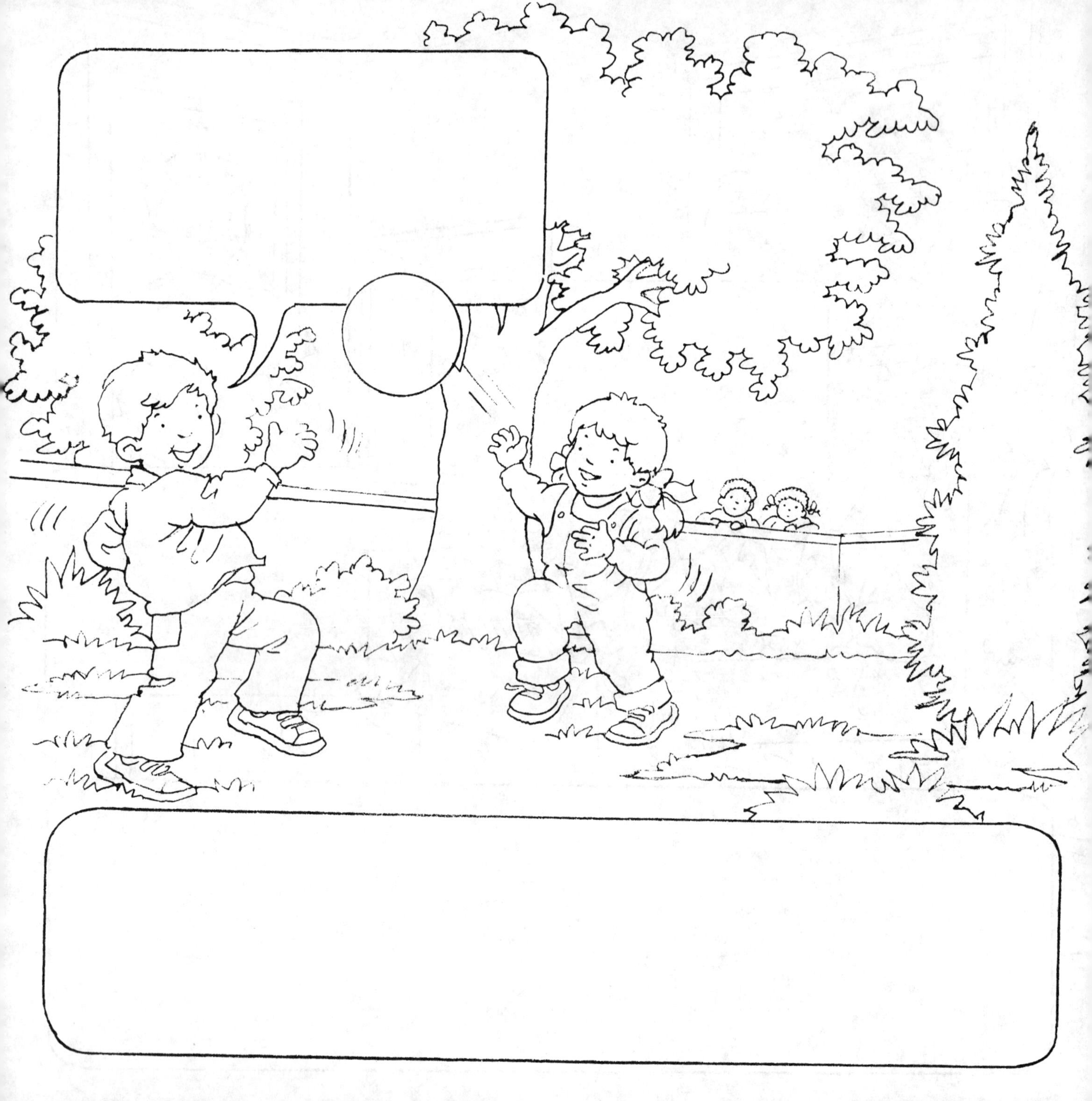

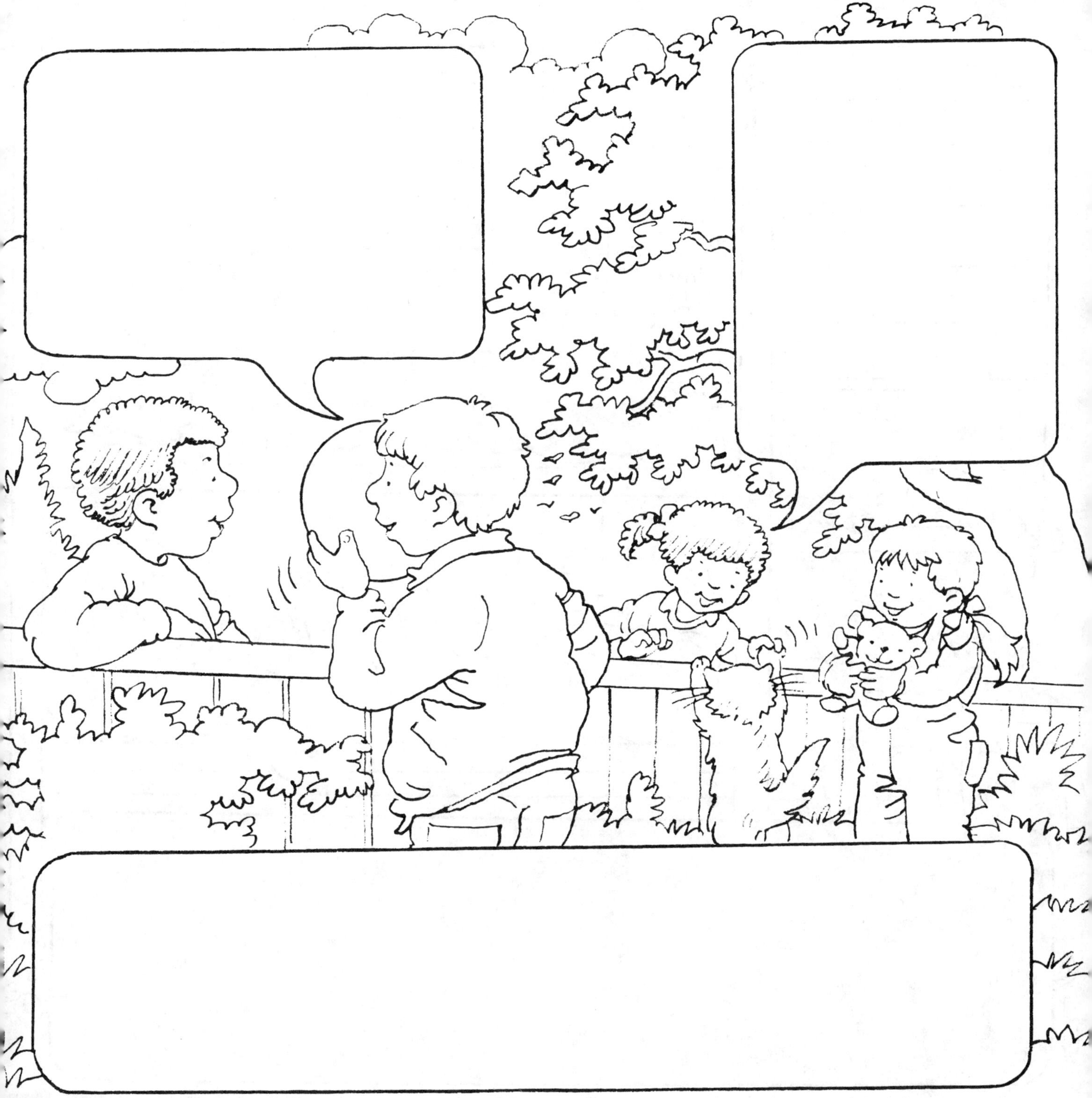

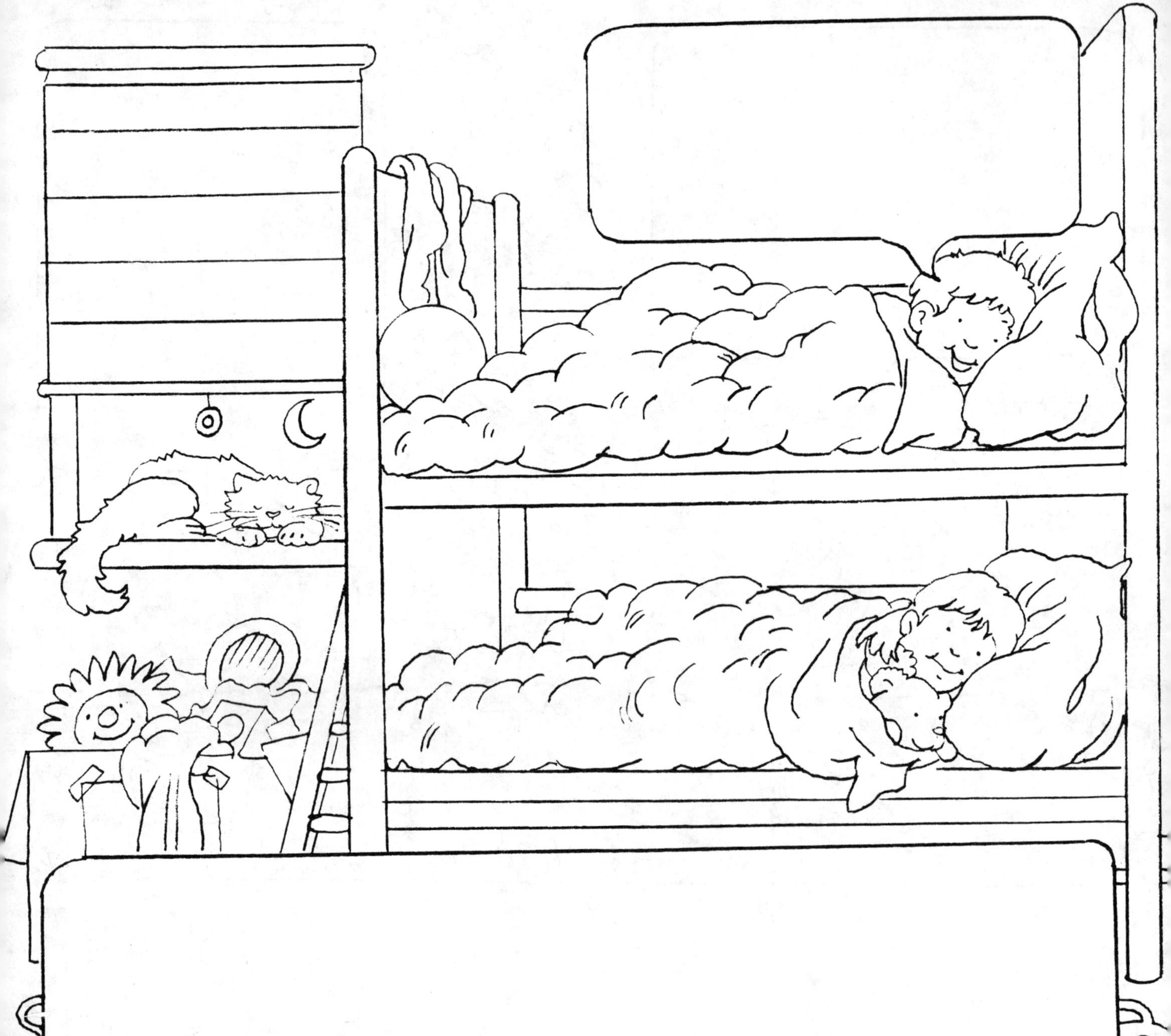